Midnight Mission

An Eco Avengers Mystery

Dawning Press
326 South Pacific Coast Highway, Ste. 209
Redondo Beach, CA 90277

www.dawnwynne.com

For more information or to book an event online or in person contact Dawning Press at
dawn@dawnwynne.com.

Library of Congress Control Number 2020908232

ISBN 978-0991614431

Printed in the United States of America

Midnight Mission

An Eco Avengers Mystery

Dawn Wynne

Illustrated by
Maria Hecher

DAWNING PRESS / LOS ANGELES

For Dad and Mom, who always believe in me even when I doubt myself

Special thanks to Jane Roseman for her keen attention to detail

Chapter 1

Neighborhood Watch

Blue Hills is a typical suburban neighborhood, clustered with well-manicured cookie-cutter homes where neighbors walk dogs, kids skateboard along sidewalks, and squirrels race across the street dodging cars. From the outside, it looks like any other suburban town, except in springtime, when vibrant blue Himalayan Poppies bloom. Visitors flock to Blue Hills, crowding the streets to view the poppies covering the ground like a warm, blue blanket.

On any given day, residents encounter the not so ordinary neighborhood mascots: Frankie, the black and white tuxedo cat; Mindy, the tri-colored Australian Shepherd; and Jagger, an average backyard raccoon. They belong to no one and everyone.

As the sun descends, Frankie, Mindy, and Jagger saunter around the block, exploring their meal options. Mr. Harmon, the neighborhood grandfather, usually initiates the morning meal for the town's animal friends. A typical breakfast consists of leftover meat and a bowl of warmed milk. The three stop and give their best "please feed me I'm starving" look.

"Sorry friends, you'll have to come back in the morning for breakfast."

Mindy hangs her head, while Frankie and Jagger whimper. No such luck here.

Next stops are Mrs. Lupia and Ms. Carter who fight over which one can provide the best dinner served on their finest china. The pack approaches Mrs. Lupia's porch first. Tonight, the menu includes grilled salmon served over jasmine rice accompanied by a bowl of fresh, dry chicken kibble she dehydrates herself.

"Salmon, my favorite," Frankie mumbles using his big head to push the two larger animals out of the way.

"Take it easy Frankie boy. There's enough for everyone," Mindy reassures.

"I hate salmon and dry crunchies," chimes Jagger. "I'm going over to Mrs. Carter's."

"Wait up," Frankie says as he gulps down the last bit of salmon and runs after Jagger.

"I guess I'll eat the kibble then," Mindy shrugs. "More for me."

Mindy finishes her meal and meanders next door to Ms. Carter's house. Frankie licks the last bit of turkey giblets while Jagger lies on his back rubbing his belly. Ms. Carter, a single forty-something lawyer, deems the neighborhood animals to be a nuisance but has resorted to feeding them because she hates to waste food. She would rather the gnarly delinquents receive the food than to toss it in the garbage bin. As long as they abide by her rules, they reap the benefits of her leftover 5-star meals from the finest restaurants in town.

"Now that was a great meal," Jagger belches.

Frankie lets out his attempt at a burp, "Blep."

"You're getting better, dude. You just need a little more air in your throat."

"Blurp," Frankie sounds out with a little more force.

"Not bad," Jagger compliments. They paw high five.

"Quit fooling around, we've got work to do!" Mindy barks out orders.

Jagger and Frankie mimic Mindy's tone, "We've got work to do!"

"Listen you can go back to a life of crime or you can take our job of neighborhood patrolling seriously. There are plenty of other animals that would love to keep watch and protect the streets," Mindy scolds.

"I'm sorry." Frankie slumps his head.

"Me too," Jagger echoes.

"I heard someone was getting into Mr. Field's garbage. Probably one of those pesky tourists that have invaded our town. Maybe we should stake out there," Frankie responds.

Jagger keeps his head down and mumbles, "Um. I think they caught the culprit. Yea, they found him the other night."

"Really, how do you know? Who was it?" Frankie questions.

"Uh, I heard it was a squirrel. Yea, Scooter I think," Jagger nervously replies, fidgeting with his front paws.

"Scooter was chased away by the alley cats; I doubt he'd come back to this neighborhood." Frankie squints his eyes.

"Well, you never know. Scooter was always getting into trouble. Wouldn't surprise me. He loved tuna and probably took the empty cans."

"How do you know the tuna cans were missing?" Frankie interrogates.

"Uh.... well.... um.... you know.... uh," Jagger stutters. Frankie stares him down. "Okay! It was me! I took the tuna! I was hungry and you ate all the kibble, so I had to have something to keep up my energy."

"*I* ate all the kibble!" Frankie emphasizes. "You scarfed down all the steak bites!"

"Enough you two! How can we patrol the neighborhood fighting crimes if *we* are the criminals?" Mindy hollers, halting the argument. "Come on! We've got work to do. And Jagger, going forward, stay out of the garbage cans."

"Oh, Okay," Jagger grumbles.

The trio saunters down the street like three eager sheriff's deputies looking for anything out of place. They have made it their mission to keep riff-raff off the streets, specifically the rats and skunks. Jagger sniffs the ground as if searching for something. Lingering traces of the sweet poppies swirl through the air. Mindy pauses, points her nose up to the nighttime sky, and tries to sense any changes as Frankie wanders between the two, swishing his tail.

It is only a matter of minutes before Frankie and Jagger's attention wanes and they chase each other up a tall oak tree. Frankie makes it halfway up before lodging himself between two branches and hollering for help. Jagger runs back down knocking Frankie off along the way.

Frankie huffs and puffs pausing to catch his breath. Time for a break. He jumps up on an Adirondack chair conveniently located in a front yard. He turns in circles finding the perfect position and plops down, observing the other two snuffing out whatever it is they are looking for. Rolling his eyes, he takes to more important tasks. Licking his paws, he rubs them over his mouth in a circular motion. Once satisfied with his face, he takes long strokes down the length of his silky body.

"Psst," sounds from the oak tree above. Frankie exaggerates a sigh and pauses his beauty regime. With eyes narrowed, he looks up and sees only the black silhouette of a tree against a starry backdrop. Nothing else to see, his tail receives the remaining focus.

"Pssssttt."

"Who's there?" Frankie cries out.

"It's me, Azure," a bird chirps from the tree.

"Azure, why didn't you say so to begin with?"

"I didn't want to wake anyone up. Mr. Nelson throws corn nuggets at me if I sing too loudly. Those things are really hard," Azure explains.

"Corn nuggets, hmmm. I've never tried those before. Are they any good? How hard are they? Never mind, just save them for me next time," Frankie says.

"Sure thing, Frankie."

"You wouldn't happen to have any on you now, would you?" Frankie asks.

Before she has a chance to reply, Mindy and Jagger stroll over.

Mindy says, "Hi Azure. You're up awfully late. Shouldn't you be sleeping? I know you like to get an early start."

"I was at the top of the Oak Knoll path getting ready to retire when I heard a strange squeaking, a screeching noise. It was like nothing I have heard before," Azure chirps.

"Maybe it was a peacock. They can be dreadfully loud," Frankie interjects.

"No, when I went down to inspect, I saw this spider-like object moving and flapping. But it wasn't a spider because it only had 4 legs and the body was hard."

"Sounds like a cockroach to me," Jagger chimes in.

"I don't think so," Azure says. "It was bigger than that."

"Was it bigger than a bread box? Did it have fur or feathers? How big were the eyes?" Jagger fires the questions.

"I'm sorry I really don't know. I know you are on night patrol, so I wanted to alert you. I must get back to my chicks. They're expecting a nighttime feeding," Azure says as she flies away.

"Sounds like we have a mystery to solve," replies Frankie.

"I'll grab the emergency backpack," adds Jagger.

"LET'S GO, TEAM!" Mindy announces.

Chapter 2

Who Are You?

The trio sprints down the street guided only by the glimmer of light protruding from the horizon. Mindy stops at the intersection using her snout to point them in the right direction. Frankie's stomach churns as heaviness from his dinner feast sets in. Seizing an opportunity, he hops on Jagger's back. Jagger staggers from the cat's weight. He reaches back with his claws, ready for a fight, when Mindy whacks her paw against his whiskers encouraging him to keep moving. As she leads the way, ever so casually, she swishes her tail and knocks Frankie to the ground smiling to herself.

The concrete ends and is replaced by a dirt trail. The faint scent of pine lingers in the air. Mindy pauses, lifts her nose into the darkened sky, and motions the group forward. "Onward crime busters! We've got an animal to save."

Mindy, with her nose to the ground, follows the trail up the hill. Jagger jumps in and out of the blue flowers leaving a cloud of petals behind. And Frankie waddles, stopping every two feet to sniff an insect, blade of grass, or anything that resembles food. He's not hungry, but he's never been known to pass up the opportunity to eat.

"Are you sure we're going the right way? Can we stop and take a break?

My paws are killing me," Frankie whines.

"Dude, we just got started. Maybe if you laid off the kibble you would have a little more stamina. You really should do some endurance training," Jagger replies, doing a karate chop in the air. Frankie holds up a paw and Jagger attempts to knock it down but misses and lands on his back.

"If you call that stamina, I rather be lazy," Frankie laughs.

Mindy comes over, grabs Frankie by the neck, and drags him along the path. Jagger has no choice but to follow. She stops suddenly, perking her ears and rotating them towards a faint sound in the distance. "Do you hear that?" she says, dropping Frankie to the ground.

"Hear what? I don't hear anything. You sure you hear something?" Jagger asks.

"Shh! Listen," Mindy whispers. The three animals freeze, twitching their ears trying to locate the sound. A low chirp gains the trio's attention.

"I *do* hear something!" Jagger swishes his tail in excitement. Frankie crouches down and wiggles his behind getting ready to pounce on the moving target. Right before his attack, a grunt stops him.

Mindy takes charge. "Wait here and don't move," she demands. "I mean it. Not a peep, not a step. Let me check out the situation." She nudges through the tall grass, stopping periodically to let her snout and ears provide guidance. "Is anyone here?" She waits for a response. All is silent. She continues, "My name is Mindy. I'm here to help. Please tell me who you are."

Chirp, cheep, cheep.

She moves closer to the sound taking small, deliberate steps.

Hiii.

She stops suddenly, looks down, and sees what looks like a black rock. She uses her paw to push it out of the way when she hears, "No!" She jumps back.

"Oh, I'm sorry!" Mindy apologizes. "I thought you were a rock."

"Yeah, that's what most people think," the dark object replies.

"Who are you?" Mindy asks, peering closely at the grayish-black hexagon shapes covering the animal's torso.

"I'm lost," she replies, extending her wrinkled neck, exposing her black onyx eyes.

"I can see that, but what are you? You don't look like any animal I've seen around the neighborhood," Mindy says, referring to the animal's legs, that are like featherless wings. Upon closer inspection, the outline of a wrinkled, white belly resembling crumbled leather comes into focus.

By this time, Frankie and Jagger have found their way to Mindy and the mystery animal, obviously ignoring Mindy's instructions.

"What's his name? How did he get here? How old is he? What is he?" Jagger fires the questions.

"First of all, I am a she, not a he. Second, I don't have a name. And third I don't know how I got here," the creature replies. "Oh, and I am a green sea turtle."

"A sea turtle! I've never seen one up close before." Jagger presses his nose up to the hatchlings' face. Frankie mimics Jagger and stares directly into the charcoal eyes. The turtle lowers her head in fear.

Mindy grabs a twig and places it in front of the turtle thinking a little game of fetch will entice her to move. Jagger stands on his back legs and does a jiggle, while Frankie swishes his tail in sporadic movements to lure her.

Mindy tries a different approach. "Little one. It's okay. We are here to help."

Frankie catches a beetle and places the limp insect in front of her shell. "Here's a little snack. I'm sure you must be hungry."

Slowly, cautiously, the hatchling extends her head and takes a bite out of Frankie's offering. She immediately spits it out. "Ugh! That's disgusting."

"Your loss." Frankie shrugs and uses the opportunity to snatch up the beetle in one gulp.

"We should give you a name," Mindy suggests. "What do you want to be called?"

"What about Tina or Rita or Sabrina? Maybe Barb or Maria," Jagger rattles off. Mindy tries to cut him off, but Frankie simply replies, "Shelly."

"Shelly. I like that." The little turtle perks up. "Shelly," she repeats trying out her name.

"You are a long way from the sea. How did you get here?" Mindy questions.

"I don't know. I just remember my mom telling us that when we were ready to leave our shells all we had to do was follow the light and it would guide us to the water. There were so many lights I didn't know where to go. I tried to follow, but everywhere I turned I saw bright lights. I kept crawling and going towards the light, but suddenly the light disappeared, and I didn't know where I was. I was afraid to stop. Loud swishing sounds and huge rolling objects whizzed by me. I couldn't hear the ocean anymore. So, I just kept walking, and eventually I couldn't hear anything."

"You are quite far from the ocean, but we can help you get back home," Mindy says.

"I'm not sure. I don't know you."

"Let me introduce myself. I'm Frankie." The tuxedo feline bows to her.

"I'm Jagger, raccoon extraordinaire." He pirouettes and trips over his leg.

"And I'm Mindy." The shepherd extends her paw to shake.

Shelly is still not sure she can trust this strange group. "Why do you want to help?"

"We are part of the neighborhood crime busters. It's our job to protect the city and help citizens," Mindy explains.

"Yeah, stick with us and we'll get you back to the water in no time," Jagger confirms.

Shelly stares and studies each set of piercing eyes. She shrugs and reluctantly agrees to follow the herd.

"It's a long way back. I think we need to rest up for the night and get a start in the morning after a hot breakfast," Frankie replies.

"We don't have time to lollygag around, Frankie. We need to get her back with her siblings so she can learn to swim and catch food," Mindy responds.

Frankie drops to the ground, groaning and moaning, "I have to eat. I can't make that journey on an empty stomach. Oh, so hungry."

Jagger rolls his eyes. "Get a grip a dude. We just had dinner."

"Frankie, we have a job to do and your well-endowed stomach is going to have to wait," Mindy chides. "Let's get going team!"

Jagger takes off needing no other invitation. Frankie follows dragging his paws.

"Jagger, you're going in the wrong direction!" Mindy warns.

He changes directions and charges down the trail. Mindy quickly follows leaving Frankie and Shelly behind. Shelly flips her fins and slides on her tummy, but for each stroke, she only gains an inch at a time. Frankie waddles not far behind Shelly, grumbling and complaining.

Five minutes elapse before Mindy and Jagger realize it's just the two of them. They wait and wait and wait until finally, the sluggish duo emerges.

"At this rate, we won't make back to the coast until next year. You two are going to have to step it up," Mindy demands. Shelly bursts into tears. "I'm sorry Shelly. I didn't mean you. Let's think of another plan."

"We can use the backpack as a saddle, and she can ride on my back," Jagger suggests.

"Good thinking!" Mindy places the backpack straps through Jagger's arms and puts the little turtle on his back. Within seconds Frankie uses Jagger's tail as a ladder and joins Shelly.

"Oh no! I didn't agree to carry your fat rump on my back!" Jagger protests, shaking Frankie off.

"I'm not fat! You owe me an apology!" Frankie demands.

"No time for fighting, carry on," Mindy urges. Jagger gives in and starts back down the trail. Frankie wastes no time rummaging in the backpack while trying to keep pace next to Jagger. He finds a stale piece of seaweed and savors every bite.

Chapter 3

Let's Roll

Moments later, the group, which now includes a turtle, returns to the neighborhood settling in front of Mrs. Lupia's house. "Okay we are going to need provisions for our journey," Mindy announces. "Jagger you get the snacks. Frankie, you get some helmets. And I'll find a map. Shelly you wait right here for us."

"Helmets, what do we need helmets for?" questions Frankie.

"We might be covering some rough terrain, so I want us to be prepared for anything. It's better to be overprepared than underprepared," Mindy explains.

They take off in different directions. Jagger heads to Mr. Harmon's garbage can. He knocks it over simply by jumping in. *Bang, bang, boom.*

"Shh!" Mindy hushes. Jagger gives her the ok sign and continues rummaging through, throwing out paper products while searching for food.

Frankie saunters over to Ms. Carter's house. He hops over the back fence and explores her garden shed. Shovels, rakes, hoes—nothing of use here. A watering can sits on the top shelf of a metal plant stand. He leaps to the top, but the weight of his body topples the shelf over, sending the can and a series of clay pots crashing to the ground.

Ms. Carter rushes from the house in her pajamas and sleep mask waving a spatula. "Get out of here you scoundrels! Scat!" She swats at the darkness. Frankie narrowly escapes, but not before taking some empty soil sacks and the china food bowls still sitting on the porch.

Within minutes the crew returns to the Lupia's driveway and share their findings. Jagger produces a box of goldfish crumbs, a half-eaten can of chili, and a carton of soured milk. Mindy shares an old, discarded tablet left in a donation box. Frankie proudly reveals the plastic soil bags. He claws a hole in one of the bags and places it over his body.

"Ta-da! Raincoats," he explains, giving one to Jagger to wear. He licks the dried fish flakes from the china bowl before distributing to each animal and instructing them to place on their heads to use as helmets.

"Wow this is cool dude." Jagger admires his transformation. He butts heads with Frankie testing out the ceramic helmet. They circle each other and throw a few friendly punches before Mindy steps in and redirects their attention.

Mindy whips out a newspaper she snagged from the driveway of a vacant house. She unrolls the newspaper and places Shelly on the edge to keep it from rolling back. Scanning through the articles she eventually finds a street map from the real estate section. She studies it carefully mapping out a route.

"Looks like we are five miles from the ocean. If we cross the highway and follow it to the Langston Bridge, we can catch the river which will lead us to the coast."

"It's five miles away!" Frankie protests.

"It's cold and dark," confers Jagger.

"There could be dangerous animals lurking."

"And my night vision isn't the greatest."

Frankie and Jagger look at each other, shrug their shoulders, and simultaneously say, "Let's roll!"

With a plan in place and a fully provisioned backpack, they begin their five-mile journey. Shelly resumes her place on Jagger's back, while Frankie, fueled with energy from the last licks of the caked-on fish, trots along next to Mindy. They wind through the suburban streets, cross the intersections of downtown, and within an hour make it to the freeway.

"Okay kids, make sure your helmets are secured. We are going to have to make a run across four lanes in five seconds," Mindy says.

Jagger shakes his head. "No way, no way, no way. I'm not crossing that death trap. At a minimum we need a crossing guard."

"Maybe we should just go back," Shelly timidly responds.

"Absolutely not," Mindy barks. "We are not quitters. We can do this! We'll go in pairs. Jagger you take Shelly. Cross one lane at a time. Frankie and I will follow behind you."

"Why do we have to go first? You're the head honcho with the map. I think we should follow you," Jagger asserts.

"You're the fastest and most skilled. We will watch how you navigate and take our lead from you," Mindy responds.

Jagger stands up taller and pats his chest upon hearing the compliment.

"Great. It's settled," Frankie says while jumping on Mindy's back.

"Oh no you don't!" Mindy snaps at Frankie. "I am not your taxi. You've got four perfectly good legs."

"Shelly and I have short legs. Plus, we will be more stealth-like if it's only one figure darting across the traffic," Frankie purrs as he rubs up against Mindy, batting his emerald green eyes. Mindy shakes her head, knowing he is right.

"Fine, but keep your claws retracted," Mindy insists. Frankie swiftly jumps on her back flashing a Cheshire grin.

Jagger stands on his hind legs, peering out to oncoming traffic. "Hold tight Shelly!" A truck whizzes by, almost knocking him down. He regains his balance and looks again. A steady stream of cars flies by flashing their blinding lights. "You can do it, you can do it," he mumbles to himself. "No, I can't. No, I can't," he counters. "Think Jagger, think. Use your raccoon brain." He paces back and forth as he comes up with an idea.

The backpack slides off causing Shelly to somersault away from Jagger. He rummages through until he finds a compass. He holds it up, tilting it back and forth, taking a step in one direction, only to change his mind and move in the opposite direction. After a couple of attempts to calibrate, he tosses the compass. He returns to the backpack and pulls out a protractor, calculating angles. That clearly does not work, so out comes a measuring tape.

He measures the length of his body, the girth of his waist, and the circumference of his head. He scrunches his brows and scratches his head. What next? The tape measure extends across the first lane. As it reaches the dotted white line, a bus zooms past taking the object with it.

Before Jagger has a chance to come up with another ridiculous scheme, Frankie rappels off Mindy, flies through the air with legs spread wide, and lands on the hood of a truck. Upon impact he immediately resumes the forward motion and jumps to the next lane landing on a compact car. Without hesitation, he leaps onto a van and then a station wagon before taking his final jump into a ditch.

The three remaining animals stare in amazement with their jaws hanging open.

"Well, that's a hard act to follow," says a stunned Mindy.

"Who knew he had it in him?" Jagger replies.

"We're definitely not following that plan. We're going to have to take it one lane at a time." Mindy looks left, then right, and left again. Car after car passes, leaving no time to make it across all four lanes in one sweep. "Jagger you stay right next to me and Shelly whatever you do, don't let go." Jagger puts the "saddle" backpack on and kneels for Shelly to resume her place.

Jagger closes his eyes. "I can't look."

"It's okay. Just stay calm and do what I do," Mindy orders. She places a paw onto the asphalt and quickly withdraws it as a minivan passes. Before she can regain her composure, Jagger, eager to stay close, bumps into her and she simultaneously jumps causing her to land in the first lane. With no other choice, she darts ahead with Jagger on her tail and Shelly hanging on to the backpack for dear life. They make it to the first white line and notice a semi-truck headed straight for them. "Now!" she hollers, and they bolt across the second lane. Mindy crouches down to make herself appear smaller. "Stay low," she orders. "And don't bump me again!" She carefully stands to survey the next lane.

"Okay, boss," Jagger replies. But as soon as his words are out a SUV approaches, clips his tail, and pushes him into Mindy. They topple over and spin around headed in the opposite direction. Shelly grips as hard as she can to prevent from falling off. "We're going the wrong way!" Jagger screeches.

"I know that!" she shouts back. Mindy immediately whips herself back around, grabs Jagger by the tail, and leaps across the second lane. She glances to the left and sees the next set of vehicles quickly approaching. She knows she must decide fast.

"I can't look!" Jagger stutters as he closes his eyes.

Taking no other chances, she bounds the final two lanes pulling Jagger along by his tail. Jagger rolls off into the ditch sending his ceramic bowl helmet flying into oncoming traffic. They watch as it shatters into hundreds of pieces.

"Weeee! That was fun!" Shelly squeals.

"Where's Frankie?" Mindy asks. Jagger picks himself up and begins searching for the black and white cat. It doesn't take long to find him curled up in a ball a few feet away.

"Is he alive?" Jagger questions. He picks up a stick and pokes him. When he doesn't move, he pokes him a little harder. Frankie groans.

As Frankie comes to and opens his eyes, he is staring straight up into the indigo, cloudless sky. "Am I in heaven?"

The rest of the gang approaches and stands over Frankie. "Mindy, Jagger.... Shelly...are you in heaven too?" he questions.

"No, you're in a ditch after hurling yourself across four lanes of traffic," Mindy explains.

"Hallelujah! I still have seven of my lives left," Frankie rejoices. "I sure could use some nourishment after that traumatic experience."

The group stares at Frankie. They recuperate in silence until their breathing returns to normal. Shelly is the first to speak. "Do you think we can continue?" her meek voice reverberates.

"I think we've rested enough. Jagger, get out the map and let's see where we need to go next," Mindy orders.

"Map, you want me to read the map? Listen, I work better off of a scent. Give me a T-bone and I can take you to the moon," Jagger replies.

Mindy seizes the map from the backpack. "Seriously do I have to do everything?" She tugs at the paper and studies it. "Looks like we follow the highway to the bridge. From there we can make it to the river which should take us to the ocean. Alright let's go!"

Chapter 4

Seeing Stars

Mindy and Jagger take the lead trotting along the graveled edge of the highway. Their feet saunter in sync like a choreographed dance routine.

"Left, left, left, right, left," Jagger takes on the role of an Army sergeant, swaying his arms to match his stride.

Frankie stumbles to get up. "Whoa. I'm so dizzy. I think I have a concussion."

Shelly approaches Frankie with wide eyes. "Are you okay Frankie?"

"I don't think so, the sky is spinning." He dramatically wobbles.

"Hey guys, I think Frankie needs help," Shelly replies in her sweet voice. Mindy and Jagger are too far ahead to hear anything.

"Oh, aww, so dizzy," Frankie wails.

"Help. We need help," Shelly commands only a fraction louder than her previous attempt.

Meanwhile, Frankie moans even louder, "OHHH! AHHH! OHHHHH!"

"HELP!" Shelly blurts. This time it's loud enough to be heard a mile away, shocking Frankie into silence.

"Did that sound come out of you?" he questions. "Who would have thought you had that in your tiny body?"

Mindy and Jagger rush back to see the emergency.

"What's wrong buddy? You okay? What's going on? Should we take him to the vet? Maybe we should call an ambulance."

Mindy simply raises her paw to quiet Jagger.

"Frankie are you in pain?"

"Dizzy, so dizzy," he responds, slurring his words.

Mindy holds up her paw. "How many claws am I holding up?"

Frankie squints and replies, "Four I think."

"Good. What is your name?" she asks.

"Frank Sinatra III."

"How old are you?" she quizzes.

"I will be three years old on May the third," he proudly states.

Mindy rolls her eyes. "Okay, I think you are going to be just fine. Try to stand up."

"Oh no I can't. I don't have it in me. So weak." He rolls onto his back splaying all four legs straight out like a flat pancake. "Oh," he groans.

"I know what will help," Jagger announces and hops into the ditch.

They eagerly await Jagger's return. Minutes go by and still no Jagger. Even Shelly isn't this slow. Shelly inches closer to Frankie and rubs his tummy. "Aw that feels good," he says.

Ten minutes have passed when Jagger sprints back with a limp, green object hanging from his mouth.

"Hey buddy. I found you something to eat." Jagger proudly drops a decapitated lizard on his stomach.

"Yikes!" Frankie squeals and jumps two feet in the air. "What is that?"

"It's a lizard," Jagger states, pleased with himself.

"I can't eat that. It's still warm," Frankie replies with a scowl.

"You're a cat. That's what cats eat. Besides, do you know how long it took me to catch that? I had to sit still for six minutes trying not to scratch my tail."

Frankie shakes his head and waddles to remove himself away from the decimated creature.

"Looks like you are all better now Frankie. Let's get moving. We have to make it to the bridge by midnight," Mindy orders.

Shelly hangs her head and slyly fishes out a lone goldfish cracker at the bottom of the backpack. She places it under her flipper and passes it to Frankie. "Here you go," she mutters under her breath.

He swallows it whole, "Thank you Shelly! You are the best friend a cat could ask for."

"Really?" she questions.

"Absolutely! We are BFF's now."

Mindy takes the lead, keeping her head to the ground following the scent to the river, while her ears track the whirls and whooshes of nearby cars. Shelly resumes her spot on Jagger's backpack saddle, and Frankie brings up the rear swaying his torso as he shuffles behind.

The buzz of the freeway fades as Mindy maneuvers the crew down an embankment. They push and stomp their way through weeds and tall grasses. Away from the blinding road, they rely on instincts to guide them through a now opaque sky. Frankie's black fur blends in with the atmosphere. Only his white muzzle is visible in between the blades of grass. Jagger jumps over the clusters as if they are hurdles. The distant whir of the highway is replaced by the constant buzz of crickets and an occasional snort from the snoring

Shelly. They trek on in silence, forging ahead for the next few hours.

As the moon emerges, a steel bridge comes into sight. "There it is! I see it! The bridge," Jagger hops up and down jolting Shelly awake.

"Great work team," Mindy graces them with a rare smile. "All we need to do is scale down to the river and it will lead us to the sea."

Jagger sheds the backpack and pulls out a can opener, a stapler, and a safety pin. He grabs the can opener and fiddles with the handles, opening and closing them while trying to turn the crank. "Ouch!" he exclaims, catching his paw on the gear. He tosses it over the bridge. He surveys the metal beams looking at it from every angle through the "lens" of the safety pin. Not satisfied, he tosses it and returns to the backpack and claims a piece of yarn. "I think we can use the stapler as a hook and tie the yarn around our bodies. I'll rappel down first and throw the string back up to you—"

"Jagger come on down," echoes through the air.

Looking around he realizes he is alone. He approaches the edge of the bridge and sees Mindy and Shelly already at the bottom.

"Wait...how did you get down there?" a baffled Jasper replies.

"We just climbed down," Shelly announces with a wide grin.

Jagger furrows his brows and tilts his head. He remains paralyzed.

"All you have to do is scoot down backward, rung by rung. Just like a ladder," Mindy explains.

"Okay," Jagger says with hesitation. "You know I really don't like heights."

"I know you can do it, Jagger," Shelly squeaks out. "One step at a time. We'll be here for you."

Jagger forces his shaky legs to move toward the edge of the bridge. He clings to the first rail with all four paws. "No, no, no, I can't do this."

"Don't think, just step on one bar at a time. And don't look down," Mindy instructs.

"Breathe Jagger. You can do this. One step at a time," Jagger repeats to himself. He stretches his hind right leg to the next rail and removes his shaky right paw to grab the lower metal brace. He remains motionless and crippled in this position. "I'm stuck, I can't move."

"Take your left arm and leg and move it down to the next bar," Mindy replies.

With his eyes closed, Jagger swiftly grabs the lower bar with his left extremities. The force of the motion causes him to lose traction of the right grip. He dangles precariously keeping grip only with his front, left paw.

"Yikes!" Shelly screams. Mindy quickly covers her mouth knowing it will only panic Jagger even more.

"You got this. Carefully swing your body to the bridge and use your right paw to grab a hold of the rung," Mindy advises.

Jagger follows Mindy's instructions and regains stability. His racing heart and sweaty paws make it difficult to keep his grip. Slowly, step by step, rung by rung, he listens to Mindy's directions and climbs his way down the structure. As he approaches the final few feet, he gives in to his slippery paws and slides to the bottom landing with a thud.

Shelly flaps her way as fast as she can to the grey heap heavily panting on the ground. "You did it! Way to go Jagger!" Shelly high fives. Jagger weakly raises a paw to return the gesture.

They give Jagger a few minutes to catch his breath and recover. As the group begins the next leg of the route, Shelly pauses. "Where's Frankie?" They look around and realize Frankie is nowhere to be seen.

Chapter 5

This is Bad

"When was the last time someone saw Frankie?" Mindy inquires.

"I don't know, he's always behind me," Jagger uttered.

Shelly hangs her head. "I fell asleep and didn't see much of anything. I'm sorry."

"Frankie! Frankie! Fraaaankieeee!" they all shout at once, pause, and continue again, "FRANKIE! Frankster!! FRANK!!"

"Oh no, this is bad, this is really bad." Jagger paces back and forth.

"What are we going to do? What if he was swallowed by a coyote? Or maybe he fell in a trap. Bats could have snatched him up. With that dark fur they might think he's one of them. I don't even think he has his rabies shot up to date."

"Calm down. Hysterics are not going to help Frankie," Mindy admonishes. "Did anyone see Frankie come down the bridge?"

The turtle and raccoon shake their heads in denial.

"We know he was on the path as we left the highway," Mindy thinks out loud. "But I don't remember seeing him once we got to the bridge."

"Me either," confers Jagger.

"I can climb back up and look for him," offers Shelly.

"I think it's best if we all stay here," Mindy directs.

Jagger continues to pace as Mindy finds a tree and plops down.

"How can you sit at a time like this?" interjects Jagger.

Mindy simply holds up a paw to silence him. She connects her index finger and thumb, forming a circle, and quietly begins to hum *ohm, ohm, ohm*. Jagger tilts his head with a blank look. Frowning, he walks away.

Meanwhile, Shelly comes up with a plan to leave a food trail for Frankie to smell his way back to them. She scours the path and collects a few wild berries left to rot on the ground. Piece by piece, she places fragments of the dried fruit composing a dot to dot maze. Surely, this will lead him to the group.

Jagger mutters and mumbles to himself as he marches back and forth wearing a path in the weeds. With hunched shoulders he bites his claw nails. "What should we do? Where could he be? Think Jagger, think."

"MEOW!" reverberates through the air. All three animals stop and look up to the top of the bridge.

"Frankie!" they shout in unison.

A disheveled Frankie appears, twigs caught in his whiskers, burrs entwined in his tail and clumps of mud stuck to his once silky coat. His chest heaves up and down. "Thanks for waiting. Nice to know I could have died, and no one would have noticed," he replies in between gasps.

"Oh, little buddy! I thought you were dead!" Jagger cries.

"You all were moving so fast. I tried to keep up. I twisted my ankle in a gopher hole. I had to fight a bird over a berry and then a snake almost took me out. I barely escaped before a pack of wild dogs chased me up a tree. And then I almost passed out from malnourishment," Frankie huffs and puffs. The gang rolls their eyes.

"Okay. Come down and join us so we can keep up our schedule," urges Mindy.

"I don't know if I have the energy to make it. I'm pretty wiped out after defending myself. And I haven't had a decent meal in three hours."

Shelly picks up a piece from her berry trail. "Here you go—"

In one fell swoop, Frankie scales down the bridge and swipes the morsel, swallowing it whole. Surprised, but not entirely shocked, the three animals just stare at the bedraggled cat.

Finally, Mindy speaks, "Great. We're all together again and now we can help Shelly get back to her home.

All we have to do is follow the river and it will lead us to the ocean."

☆☆☆

They follow Mindy's lead at a slower pace. Heavy legs reluctantly drag along the ground. Jagger takes pity on Shelly and scoops her up and places her on his backpack. Step by step they move, much like a slow-motion film. Their eyes drop and quickly flit back open willing them to stay awake.

As they venture deeper into the grassy unknown, their breathing becomes laborious. Shallow breaths in and quick exhales echo back and forth. They find a machine-like automation to their steps. Step, breathe, step, breathe, step, breathe. *Crack*! They freeze, as the fur on their backs stands straight up forming a mohawk.

Mindy is the first to swivel her head towards the cracking vibration while the rest of her body remains motionless. Jagger's shaky legs only allow him to turn ten degrees to the right. His heart pounds so hard Shelly bobs up and down trying to keep her grip while remaining still. Frankie mimics their frozen stances and looks back and forth between the dog and raccoon. He shrugs and continues to shuffle his feet ahead of the paused crew. He takes a few steps when the *crack* reverberates again.

"Ahh!" Mindy and Jagger jump a foot in the air. Shelly flies off Jagger and lands on her back next to them.

"Sure could use some help here. I've been through several traumatic experiences and I'm running on fumes," Frankie whines after stepping on a fallen tree branch. Mindy and Jagger clench their teeth and shoot daggers at Frankie, daring him to say another word. Frankie knows better and utters a final grunt before continuing in the queue.

Jagger flips over Shelly and returns her to his back. Onward they continue.

Chapter 6

The Final Leg

The river winds through the dense trees, occasionally allowing glimpses of the moon to penetrate, offering a brief illumination from the darkness. They travel in silence except for the occasional snore from Shelly or a grunt from Frankie. A clearing appears as the moon positions itself directly above them.

Frankie is the first to break the silence. "Mindy, can we *please* take a break?"

"Yeah boss, my back is getting chafed from this backpack," Jagger chimes in.

"Alright," Mindy sighs, "but just a quick rest. Shelly needs to make it before sunrise so she can join the next set of hatchlings' journey to the sea."

Jagger shrugs off the backpack and immediately jumps into the river, frolicking and dancing as water erupts like a volcano spewing its droplets, creating rippling waves. He hums and jiggles, restoring energy from the crisp water.

Shelly cautiously approaches the river's edge and dips a flipper into the stream. She uses her aquatic foot to splash, delighting in the ensuing ripples. Instinct takes over and she flaps all four flippers propelling her into the lazy current. She is a natural: diving, bobbing, floating, and gliding through the stream.

Frankie hobbles to join them, but there is no way he is immersing his body in that ice bath. Instead, he delicately places one paw in the water, just enough to wet his pads and assess the taste. Passing his taste test, Frankie laps up the liquid as fast as he can. He drinks and drinks and drinks. Bloated and weighted, he makes his way to a rock and plops down. He eventually lifts his heavy head to remove the burrs, twigs, and mud from his earlier encounters.

Mindy joins the group carrying an evening snack. Jagger leaps out of the water while Shelly continues to enjoy her newly acquired swimming skills. Frankie needs no other invitation to join.

"Duck pate! Where did you get this?" Frankie squeals.

"I brought it," Mindy simply states.

"What? You had this with you the whole time? Why have you been letting me starve?"

"If I pulled out all the food at once you would have gobbled it up in five seconds flat. We needed to ration our provisions."

"I can have self-control when I need to. That is really cruel," Frankie pouts. As soon as the words are out of his mouth, he devours the pate. "Umm, yum, so good."

Jagger approaches the bowl and takes two bites before Frankie nudges him away with his bulky head. Mindy motions Jagger aside where she has another bowl of the leftover chili covered with the sour milk previously packed waiting for him. Jagger gobbles the garbage can food. Shelly nibbles on a piece of grass she found floating in the stream. Mindy patiently waits for Frankie and Jagger to finish before she steps in and laps up the scarce remains stuck to the edges of the bowls.

"Now that was a good snack," Frankie says as he plops to the ground rolling on his back from side to side. Jagger joins him basking in the soothing "massage." Feeling left out, Shelly emerges from the water and observes their behavior. She pushes her flippers off the dirt to get a rocking motion. After several attempts she gains enough momentum to push herself directly onto her back. Her flippers flail in the air. What is so great about this?

"Help!" she panics. "Get me up!"

Frankie and Jagger abruptly stop and rush to flip her over.

"I don't know what you all see in that. That was horrible. Everything was upside down." Shelly shakes.

"You have a shell, so you probably don't need to scratch like we do," Jagger explains. "It feels so good."

"If you say so."

"That's enough resting. Let's regroup and keep moving," Mindy advises.

The group resumes their formation and treks ahead. They follow in silence keeping the river to their right. Through scratchy weeds, under dangling tree branches, wading in shallow water they travel continuously as the sky deepens into the night. Mindy is the first to speak.

"Okay, gang, we need to get Shelly to the sea before the sun rises so she can follow the current and meet up with the rest of the turtles."

"What happens if we don't make it by sunrise?" Jagger asks.

"Her family will be too far out in the ocean and she won't be able to reach them."

"Let's go then," Frankie chimes in.

Once again, the group carries on.

"*Over the river and through the woods, to grandmother's house we go*," Jagger sings.

"We're not going to grandmother's house you dope," Frankie retorts.

"It's how the song goes. And technically Shelly might be meeting up with her grandmother," Jagger defends himself.

Jagger starts in on a different tune, "*The wheels on the bus go round and round, round and round—*"

"What bus? We're walking you dummy!"

"I'm trying to keep us awake. "*The ants go marching one by one, hurrah, hurrah. The ants go marching one by one, hurrah, hurrah*," Jagger switches yet again.

Frankie grabs two nearby leaves and shoves them in his ears, muting Jagger's singing. Mindy and Shelly join in the tune, anything to keep them awake. The minutes linger as the night sky sets in darkening with each step they take. Soon they are cocooned by the sapphire atmosphere. Glimmers of light reflecting from the moon onto the river provide brief glimpses of illumination here and there. As their weariness sets in, a faint *whoosh* chimes in the distance. On cue, the gang stops and perks up their ears, rotating and twisting like antennas trying to receive a signal.

"That's it," Shelly speaks up, "that's what I heard when I came out of my shell."

"We are close now," Mindy states.

"Thank goodness. My paws are raw, not to mention my back is killing me," Frankie complains.

"Your back?" Jagger groans, "I'm the one carrying the paw pack and a sea turtle all night."

"No time for arguing and complaining," Mindy chides. "We're on a mission." She nudges them forward and this time takes up the rear to keep them marching ahead.

The river widens and the ocean waves get louder and stronger. Damp, salty air penetrates their nostrils. Frankie licks his lips thinking about an ocean full of seafood. Sensing how near they are, they pick up the pace. Shelly fights to remain on Jagger's back. Soon the dirt path transforms into tiny granules of sand. One final push over a mound and they see it: miles of indigo waves, topped with white foam that disperses as it spreads over smooth sand. *Crash, whoosh, shh* the waves speak.

"We're here!" Shelly slides off Jagger's back.

"You are home now little one," Mindy confirms. "All you have to do is let the waves take you out and follow your instincts from there."

"I can't go out alone. I need to wait for my brothers and sisters," Shelly counters.

Jagger raises his brows. "Brothers and sisters?"

"Yeah, another group will be hatching soon. We all need to travel together," she flaps making her way to the concave bowl on the shoreline.

Mindy and Jagger follow as Frankie digs his feet deeper into the sand. "I didn't sign up for this. We agreed to help her find her way back to the ocean and we did. Job done; case closed."

"Don't be ridiculous, Frankie. We've come this far. We can spare a few extra minutes to make sure she's reunited," Mindy scolds.

Frankie plops down and refuses to move. Jagger and Mindy breeze past him kicking sand over his body as they follow Shelly to the indented sandpit. Three dark eyes peer in. Dozens of ping pong sized eggs are neatly stacked on top of each other. All is quiet.

"I guess we wait." Mindy stretches on her stomach, resting her head on her paws. Jagger curls on his side, while Shelly hovers over the edge, eyes wide, willing her siblings to arrive.

Chapter 7

Trouble Over the Moon

Tap, tap, tap. Peck, peck, peck.

"Wake up! Wake up!" Shelly shrieks.

Mindy immediately jumps pointing her ears straight up in attention. Jagger rolls over, disorientated by the night sky which has not yet welcomed the morning sun. "What? Where am I? What's going on?"

"They're hatching!" Shelly announces. Even Frankie must see this. He totters over to the nest. *Crack*. A seam appears in one of the eggs. He waits, but nothing more happens. He brushes it with his paw and rolls it over as if a toy. *Crracck*. He jumps back. Cautiously, he moves closer to the egg and crouches down to eye level. *Tap, tap, tap*. A pause. *Tap, tap*. His whiskers twitch, but he keeps his body still.

"Come on, you can do it," Frankie utters in his softest voice.

Criiickk. The crack opens wider. Like an earthquake fault revealing its surface, a black hook protrudes, followed by the head of what looks like a lizard. Frankie holds his breath, keeping his eyes glued to the dark alien. An ebony flipper emerges followed by the second. *Crunch*. The egg gives way and the little creature tumbles out. It shakes its head flinging sand right into Frankie's eyes and hobbles towards Shelly.

"Hello. Hi there," she cries, flapping her fins up and down.

"Who are you?" the tiny hatchling replies.

"I'm your sister."

Within an hour the clutch of eggs has opened, and dozens of hatchlings flip flop, and rumble like a pot of boiling water. Shelly directs them to the sea. "Follow the light of the moon and stars, down the slope. That will take you to the ocean."

Black dots scatter across the sand. "Follow the light," she repeats. Some head north, others east and west, but eventually they all wiggle toward the toppling waves.

Suddenly, the moon disappears, overcome by passing clouds masking the guiding rays. The turtles continue onward but start to veer off in alternate directions. Some rotate in circles as if on a merry-go-round. Others crisscross back and forth like a ping pong match. One group veers toward the street.

"No! What's happening?" Shelly panics.

"Looks like there is a storm moving in and the clouds have covered the moon, blocking the light," Mindy states.

"Oh no. This is bad, very bad. What are we going to do?" Jagger paces, fidgeting with his paws. "We have to do something. Think Jagger, think."

"I have an idea," Mindy interrupts. Jagger, you gather the ones going toward the road. I'll get the ones headed away from the sea, and Frankie—" she stops, looking around for the tuxedo feline. "Never mind, I don't have time for his antics. Jagger follow my lead."

Her herding instincts kick in and she ushers a group back toward the water. "Here little ones, this way." *Tsst, tsst*, she presses her lips together making a clicking sound. For every group Mindy gets in the right direction, another gang heads the opposite way.

Jagger runs in circles, getting a cluster back in the right direction, only to have them turn around again. He makes himself dizzy zig-zagging back and forth like a maze. "Yo, dude, over here. No, come here. Hey! *PWEEEEEEE!*" he whistles. Everyone stops, but the hatchlings.

A blinding light suddenly appears directly parallel to the coast. "Hey, over here," echoes from the light. The hatchlings instantly maneuver themselves in the direction of the light source. They shuffle across the sand trying to gain traction. Mindy and Jagger can only follow the voice as the harsh light has created a whiteout effect, temporarily blinding their vision. They soon find their way to the origin of light. After allowing their eyes to adjust they notice

Frankie on the opposite side of a chain-linked fence. He holds the cord to a large spotlight.

"Dude, what are you doing there?" Jagger questions.

"I'm recreating the moonlight for the turtles. Obviously, your mumbo-jumbo dance moves were not working so I had to take charge."

"One slight problem genius...your "moonlight" is on the ground and not in the sky. All of the turtles are headed in this direction."

Oops! Frankie neglected to think that minor little issue through. He tugs on the cord and tries to aim the spotlight up. "Mindy, give me a paw." She ascends the chain-linked fence and jumps the remaining distance to join Frankie. She too pulls on the line, but it does not budge.

Jagger disappears but quickly returns with the backpack. He pulls out a pair of binoculars and points them toward the now concealed moon. He takes out calipers and measures various objects from the spotlight to a grain of sand, to an empty bag of crackers. A calculator appears and he starts punching in numbers, looking at the night sky and back at the spotlight. "Got it! All we need now is some sort of reflector. Then we can redirect the light."

Mindy scouts out the area. Tractors, shovels, hammers, ladders, but no reflectors.

"Hurry!" Jagger shouts from the other side of the fence, "the babies are getting close."

Mindy appears dragging a piece of sheet metal twice the length of her body. "How's this? Can we use it?"

"That will work. Excellent job!" Jagger gives a thumbs up. "I'll help you lift it and put it in front of the spotlight." In an instant, he clambers over the fence and grabs one end of the metal. They both push their body, grunting and huffing trying to move it directly in front of the light.

"Frankie, I need you to tell us which way to move the metal: up or down," Mindy instructs.

"Move it down. No, up a little. A little more down. Down more. Now up. Right. No left. Right there. No, aim it up. I think it needs to go down." The light bounces from the coast to the sky, from the nearby buildings to the endless sea of darkness.

"Frankie!"

"What? I'm trying to get the precise location. You think this is easy?" Frankie turns to leave.

Mindy tries a different tactic. "Hold on! Why don't you help Jagger since you're so strong? I'll direct the beam."

Frankie puffs up his chest and arches his back in response to the compliment. "Fine."

Mindy gets a running start and gracefully leaps over the fence. She positions herself in front of the sheet metal, "Boys angle it up and to the left. Good. Now point it down a hair. Excellent. Just a fraction to the right. Stop! That's it. Now keep it steady."

She trots over to the approaching sea turtles and herds them back in the direction of the tide. The spotlight bounces off the clouds creating a foggy replica of the moon. Light funnels a path guiding the bale of turtles to their destination. Flip, flop, flip, flop, fins totter in disunion.

Inch by inch, the black shells morph into specks and eventually disappear into the inky waters. Heads bob up and down as they are carried into the endless horizon. Shelly patiently waits for the last of her siblings to begin their journey into the lost years. Idly they float, destination unknown.

"I can't thank you enough for all of your help and kindness," Shelly bows her head.

Mindy wells up, "It has been our pleasure. Go be with your family now."

Shelly waves a final goodbye and is transported out by the current. The trio huddles together comforting each other. They watch until she blends in and becomes part of the ocean.

Sobs erupt. "She was the best friend a cat could ask for."

"I'm going to miss her snoring on my back," Jagger cries.

"I liked having another girl around," Mindy weeps. "And she was the only one who didn't complain."

"We don't complain," Jagger and Frankie reply at the same time. They drop to the ground wailing and snorting as tears soak their fur. Always the mother, Mindy consoles them as best as she can, in between her own grief. Cries turn into whimpers only to return once again to fits of bawling. Several rounds of mourning occur before exhaustion sets in. Sleep takes over. Minutes pass, maybe even hours, when they hear *tap, tap, tap.*

DAWN WYNNE

Chapter 8

It's Not Over

"Ouch," jumps Jagger. A small hatchling pecks at his paw. "Oh no, one got left behind. What are we going to do? We must help him. Let's get him to the water."

"It's me Jagger."

"How do you know my name?"

"It's me Shelly."

"No, it can't be. I must be dreaming. Pinch me."

She willingly obliges by digging her carbuncle deeper into his leg.

"OUCH!!"

Mindy and Frankie, now fully awake, rub their eyes, adjusting to the bright morning sun. "We saw you get carried out to sea. I know what I saw." Frankie shakes his head.

"I did, but I came back," admits Shelly.

"Why?" Mindy questions. "You are supposed to be with the other turtles."

"Something wasn't right. As I was riding the waves, I kept thinking about the spotlight you found and realized that's why I got disoriented. I think it was turned on the night I was born. It confused me and I went in the wrong direction."

"Are you sure Shelly? Why would the spotlight be aimed toward your nest?"

"That's what I was asking myself. Why is there even a light out here to begin with?"

Frankie chimes in, "There wasn't just a spotlight. Remember all the tools we found? They were locked up behind that fence."

"Let's go check it out," Jagger is eager to investigate.

"I'm not sure that's a good idea," Mindy hesitates. "It's locked up for a reason."

"A reason we need to find out." Frankie grabs Jagger and they bounce toward the barricaded facade. Jagger quickly scales the fence while Frankie makes it halfway up and starts huffing and puffing.

"Come on buddy. Put your back into it," Jagger encourages.

With a final grunt and push, Frankie makes it to the top and tumbles down the other side, landing with a thump on the hard soil. Jagger picks him up by the scruff of his neck and shakes him out of his disorientation. "I'll go left, you go right," instructs Jagger.

Nose to the ground, Frankie follows the scents. Jagger reverses his direction, his snout held high, scouting out the unfamiliar odors. Frankie struts a few feet and stops. Suddenly his paws dig in the dirt, slowly at first and then frantically spewing soil all around himself. He stops, sniffs, and digs a little deeper. Burying his head into the self-created hole, he pulls out a beef jerky wrapper. There's nothing left, but that does not stop him from rubbing his whiskers all over the crumpled plastic, taking in every last bit of spice associated with the savory snack. He plops to the ground and rolls, relishing in the smoky remnants of the packaging.

"Frankie you better not be taking a snack break," Jagger snaps him back to reality and he remembers his mission. *Come on Frankster, you gotta stay focused*. He shakes himself off and goes into detective mode. *Spotlight, shovels, fence...keep looking.*

Now on full alert, he looks high, low, and side to side. His search takes him only a few feet before he is stopped by a large mound of dirt. *Whoa! That's one big hill.* After a couple of attempts to climb, only to slide back down, he decides the simpler way might be to go around the pile. With a little more pep in his step, Frankie follows the base of the mound. When it ends, he turns the corner and runs into a black, rubber object. He circles the pungent mass. It is at least ten times his size. His eyes follow the base upward, higher, and higher. *I've seen this before, however, I haven't seen one this big* he mutters to himself.

To confirm his theory, he walks further south, turns west and then heads back up north and returns to his starting point. *Yep, it's a tire.*

Wanting to know more about this oversized heap of rubber, he grabs hold of one tread with his claws and pulls himself onto the tire. Paw over paw, he climbs his way to the top. He is now sheltered by a yellow, metal dome. With a quick leap, he lands onto the wheel well and climbs inside the carriage. *Holy Moly!* From this vantage point, Frankie can see piles of sandy dirt that have been cleared away leaving a flat, desolate plain.

"Woo hoo!" Frankie tries to whistle. Hearing nothing, he yells, "Jagger!!"

"Yeah, what is it?"

"You gotta come here!"

"Where are you?"

"Over here. Behind the mounds of dirt."

Jagger follows the sound of Frankie's voice. "That's it. Keep coming. Now look up."

"All I see is a heap of soil."

"Yep. Keeping walking and it will stop. Then turn left."

Jagger follows Frankie's instructions.

"Stop! Look up!" Frankie hollers down.

"You're on a skid steer."

"A skid what?" questions Frankie.

"A skid steer. It's a type of tractor used to excavate," Jagger explains.

"Excavate? What does that mean? Stop using those fancy words."

"The land is being cleared away for some reason."

Jagger vaults up the tractor and joins Frankie inside the steel-framed cab.

"Looks like someone is building something," Jagger responds.

"Building on a beach with nesting sea turtles is illegal," Frankie points out.

Jagger sniffs and rummages around. He finds an empty soda can and tosses it to the ground. A rotting apple sits on the dashboard. He offers it to Frankie, who wrinkles his nose. The apple joins the abandoned soda can.

Frankie follows Jagger's quest by searching the bottom of the vehicle. A gap between the floorboard and seat provides an opportunity to explore. His whiskers confirm he has just enough space for his head to fit. The head is the easy part. His husky body is something else. He takes a deep breath and exhales until the air is pushed out of his body. Like an army figure he pulls himself forward, scrunching his abdomen to the floor. The metal bar supporting the chair scrapes against his spine.

"Argh!"

"Suck it in big boy."

"Ugh," he pushes his hind legs giving him just enough traction to propel himself under the seat. A pencil rolls out, followed by used tissues.

"Gross!" Jagger dropkicks the snot wad outside the cabin. Frankie's paw pushes out another object. This one is a blue cylinder, paper roll. Jagger grabs it and unrolls the paper sheet.

Frankie pushes his head back the way it came in, but it doesn't fit. He turns around and tries to back out tail first. Exhaling, he flattens his body like a pancake and shimmies his rear end back and forth. No movement. His body torques and shakes like a washing machine.

"Help! Could use a paw here."

Jagger's shoulders shake and his chest heaves as he bites his lip. He folds his arms and shakes his head. He lets Frankie struggle a while before grabbing his tail and yanking him out.

Quick, shallow breaths expand Frankie's body as sweat drenches his paws. With shaky legs, he hoists his body off the ground and flicks away the moisture with a final shake. He hobbles over to the rectangular paper Jagger has laid out.

They both stare blankly at it. White lines intersect the blue background, crossing to create boxes of squares and rectangles.

"Turn it around," orders Frankie. Jagger turns the rectangle plan. Still making no sense, Jagger turns it again.

"No this way!" Frankie argues. They yell back and forth rotating and pulling the paper until they hear *rrrippp*.

"Now, you've really done it!" Jagger pounces on Frankie. Frankie defends himself by taking a swipe at Jagger with extended claws. Jagger whacks him in the head with his tail. Suddenly they both are in full force on top of each other, rolling in circles as one attached object. *Grr. Rahhh. Meowww.*

"It's all your fault!"

"You ripped the paper!"

"No I didn't, you grabbed it from me!" the two animals scream over each other.

In one abrupt motion, the momentum of their actions sends them flying from the cab toward the ground. They land with a thud just as Mindy and Shelly arrive on the scene, swirling in a halo of blue paper confetti.

Chapter 9

Time for a Plan

"What's going on here?" questions Mindy.

"We found a map," Jagger reports twitching his tail.

"No, it was a blueprint," corrects Frankie.

"Map, blueprint, same thing—"

Mindy cuts them off, "I get it. But why is it shredded into pieces?"

Jagger and Frankie stare at each other, raise their eyebrows, and shrug their shoulders.

"Never mind, just pick up all these pieces of paper."

Frankie and Jagger square off with folded arms to see who will act first.

"Don't just stand there, put it back together," Mindy barks.

Without hesitation, they arrange the fragments and fit them into place like a jigsaw puzzle. Mindy circles the fractured drawing. She sits in front of it and her ears perk up. The others wait for a reaction.

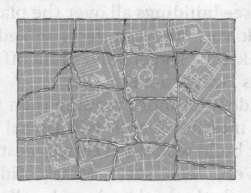

"It's a design plan," Mindy finally replies.

"A design for what?" Shelly asks.

"Well, from the looks of it, I think it's a hotel. See here is a parking lot, and that's a pool, this is a restaurant, and the large drawing is the hotel building itself." Mindy points.

"Restaurant? Where's the restaurant?" Frankie salivates.

"I knew it!" Jagger jumps in. "I told Frankie they were digging to build something."

"And I said they are not allowed to build on the beach." Frankie moves closer to Jagger with clenched paws.

"I see buildings all over the place. I think you got your facts mixed up Frankster." Jagger waves him off and turns away from Frankie.

"I do a lot more reading than you. Any internet search will reveal you can't build where sea turtles nest."

"Well, let's see," Mindy fiddles through the backpack and pulls out the tablet. She uses the voice command, "What are the building restrictions near sea turtles?"

The tablet replies, "Sea turtles are given legal protection in the United

States and its waters under the Endangered Species Act (ESA), which lists the hawksbill, leatherback, Kemp's ridley, and green turtle as endangered; the loggerhead is listed as threatened. This designation makes it illegal to harm, harass, or kill any sea turtles, hatchlings, or their eggs."

"I'm a green sea turtle," Shelly proudly announces, "but what does endangered mean?"

"It means that if people continue with their actions, there won't be any sea turtles left, they will become extinct," Mindy explains.

"Oh, that's horrible," Shelly cries.

"Don't fret little one, we're not going to let that happen." Frankie puts his arm around Shelly.

Mindy reads from a passage on the electronic screen, "Some states have passed laws to protect the species. In Florida for instance, the Marine Turtle Protection Act was passed giving state agencies the power to enforce regulations protecting turtles and their habitat. Some local governments have passed regulations to eliminate or control artificial beachfront lighting, which is known to deter females from nesting and disorient hatchlings."

"This is a serious violation! We need to call the police! Report this to the FBI! Hire a private investigator!" Jagger frantically jumps in to problem solve.

"Who is going to believe a bunch of animals that look like they were just released from the shelter?" Frankie rolls his eyes.

Shelly peers down as she speaks up. "I could go to the police."

"No offense, Shelly, but we need an army for this," Frankie states.

"Jagger is right," Mindy says.

"I am?" Jagger's voice pitches.

"We need more facts. A private investigator is our best bet. They'll take money from anyone."

"Who needs a PI when you've got us.... the...the" Frankie struggles to come up with a name for the motley crew.

"Super Sleuths!" suggests Jagger.

"Animal Rescuers," Mindy proposes.

"Crime Fighters!" Frankie chimes in.

"Dynamic Foursome."

"Awesome Animals."

"The Best!" Everyone stops and stares blankly at Jagger. Frankie opens his mouth to make a snide comment but closes it issuing his self-restraint.

"Eco Avengers," Shelly's head pops up to announce. All necks turn toward Shelly. They nod and mull over her suggestion.

"Eco Avengers...that's got a nice ring to it," agrees Jagger.

Mindy and Frankie simultaneously try out the name, "Eco Avengers, Eco Avengers."

"That settles it. Eco Avengers let's get to the bottom of this. We've got to start gathering facts. Jagger and Shelly, you head toward the ocean and gather anything that looks relevant to our case: tools, equipment, more plans. Frankie and I will survey the soil and take photos. Let's all meet back here at 1300 hours and report our findings."

"Right on boss!" Jagger high fives Mindy and takes off with Shelly bouncing on his tail.

Chapter 10

Operation Investigation

Mindy and Frankie sniff out the surrounding territory. Frankie stops to dig every few feet and Mindy uses her paw pad to snap photos from the tablet. After several minutes, Frankie stumbles on something hard. He digs and digs and comes across a metal pipe. Mindy clicks away as if this were a crime scene; well it could very well be one.

"It's a pipe!" Frankie shouts.

"Let's follow it," Mindy says.

Using their keen snouts, they maneuver across the dirt which leads them to a sewer drain.

"Okay, evidence number one, plumbing pipe," Mindy types into the handheld computer. "Keep going."

They walk only a few yards before discovering a large metal box.

"What is it?" Frankie asks.

Mindy circles the aluminum object using her nostrils to decipher the piece of equipment. The scent takes her up the box, down the side, and around the bottom. She closes her eyes and breathes.

"No time for napping. Chop, chop," Frankie pokes Mindy with his claw.

Mindy opens her eyes, "It's a generator. This must be how they are powering up the spotlight at night." She takes numerous pictures from various angles. "Let's see what else we can find."

With a bewildered tilt of his head, Frankie doesn't question and progresses forward. Lightheadedness sets in causing his legs to shake. He holds his paws in front of him and notices his fingers trembling. *When was the last time he ate?*

To stabilize his blood sugar, he hunts for food by detecting various scents. Only a few feet away he picks up on something. His ears tweak and twitch and yet again he begins to dig down, this time pulling out a red, plastic chip bag. Saliva forms on the corners of his lips. Like mad, he thrusts his head into the bag devouring any remaining bits of crumbs. The headless cat shakes his skull, but the bag remains attached to his torso. He sways and turns in circles trying to dislodge the bag. As his body contorts, he stumbles forward, heading toward an open pit.

"Frankie stop!" Mindy cries.

Unable to hear with his ears masked, he advances closer to a large hole directly in front of him.

Louder this time, "FRANKIE! STOP!"

Mindy realizes he cannot hear and bounds towards the convulsing cat. Frankie is one step away from falling into the black crater when Mindy grabs him by the scruff of the neck and pulls him back to safety. She tugs the bag off his head and puts her ear to his mouth to make sure he is still breathing. Her other paw rests on his heart searching for the steady beat.

Smiling, Frankie reaches up with both paws, grabbing Mindy's neck, and takes a bite out of her ear. He tries to initiate a round of friendly play, but Mindy pushes him off.

"Your obsession for food is going to cost you your life one day," scolds Mindy.

"It's a good thing I have seven lives left," Frankie states.

"I think you might be on your sixth Frankie. You stay here. I want to see what you almost fell into."

"No, we are a team. We stick together."

"Okay but stay by my side. No wandering off," Mindy warns.

Frankie salutes her as if she is a captain. He takes his place following her stride. When they reach the edge, Mindy holds her forward leg in front of Frankie signaling him to stop. Ever so gently, they peer their heads into the deep, dark pit. It takes a moment for their eyes to adjust, but they soon focus on metal rebar that intersects horizontally and vertically, forming what looks like squares on a checkerboard. The rods brace themselves in the rectangular hole.

"What could this be?" Mindy questions.

"It's a pool." Frankie stands tall.

"A pool? You think so?"

"Yes, remember last summer the Perkins put in a pool? They dug a hole and then put in metal sticks like these before they poured the concrete."

"You're absolutely right Frankie." Mindy enables the flash on the tablet and zooms in to take more photos to add to their growing pile of evidence. "We've got some good pictures here. We should head back to meet Jagger and Shelly."

☆☆☆

"Look at this! Check it out! See what we found!" Jagger jumps up and down greeting Mindy and Frankie. He reveals a notebook with sketches and fabric swatches. Mindy turns the page and observes a rendering of a room with a bed, two wood end tables, and a mahogany dresser. The next page reveals a balcony with wicker furniture and a glass table. Each page displays different room configurations. Canvas fabric, paint chips, and carpet samples accompany each picture.

"These must be the designs for the hotel rooms," Mindy realizes. "Great work everyone."

"Yeah, I hate the color scheme. I'm thinking cool colors would be more suitable for an ocean resort," Jagger says. They all stare at him. Shelly changes the subject.

"Did you find anything?" she asks of Mindy and Jagger.

"We found the pool site, a generator which we think is used to power the lights at nighttime, and some plumbing pipes that lead to the sewer," Frankie lists.

"What do you think, Boss? Do we have enough evidence? Can we go to the police now?" Jagger carries on.

"Hold on," Mindy urges. "We need to think this through. I'm not sure they are going to take a bunch of animals seriously. We need a human to deliver this message."

Shelly squints her eyes. "But if humans won't listen to us how do we get them to deliver the message?"

Mindy paces and nods her head up and down. "We need to get this evidence into the right hands...we could deliver this anonymously to the police...no they might think it's a bomb and destroy it." She continues to brainstorm out loud, "Maybe we show the neighbors...no, not strong enough. I guess we could—"

Frankie cuts her off, "The media."

"The media?" Mindy raises her eyebrows.

"Yes, we give our evidence to the Stillwater Herald. They are always doing environmental pieces. And then we alert Channel 4 so they bring a TV crew here and see for themselves," Frankie smiles revealing all his teeth.

"Brilliant Frankie! I am going to take pictures of everything, and we can send them to the editors and producers."

Within minutes Mindy locates the newspaper and television station websites. She composes a letter and uploads the photos through their anonymous contact form.

"Done." Mindy pushes the send button. "I guess we just wait and see now."

Chapter 11

It's Showtime

Beep, beep, beep. The quartet awakes to the grumbling and roaring of bulldozers and tractors.

"Oh no, it didn't work." Shelly covers her eyes.

"Don't worry Shelly," Frankie encourages. "It might take a while."

"I don't know how much longer I have. My family is probably in the middle of the ocean by now."

"We'll make sure you catch up to them," Jagger promises.

"In the meantime, we can stall," Mindy says. "I have an idea. They can't dig or operate machinery if animals are in the way."

The lightbulb goes on one at a time like a pinball machine lighting up each bulb. They run off, scattering in various directions. Shelly flaps her way toward the ocean. Mindy jogs toward a dump truck and Frankie heads for the skid steer. Jagger leaps toward the street.

Jagger spots a crew digging holes. He bounces and turns in front of them jiggling his rear. A constructor worker lifts his shovel and runs forward to him. Jagger immediately spins around before the shovel comes down. The second guy approaches from behind ready to take a stab. Jagger crouches low, takes a breath, and darts ahead squeezing between the man's legs. The worker looks down, then up, and side to side, trying to track the raccoon's scattered movements. Jagger weaves in between the two leaving them dizzy and breathless.

At the skid steer, Frankie scales up the tires with ease, knowing the terrain after his nightly exploration. He jumps on the shoulder of the operator. The man attempts to push Frankie off, but Frankie digs his claws in deeper. "Ouch!!" He swats at the cat, but Frankie jumps onto the steering wheel, blocking his view. He shakes his tail in the driver's face. Before the driver can grab his tail, Frankie leaps onto the floorboard and weaves himself between the pedals forcing the worker to stop.

Meanwhile, Mindy barks at a dump truck driver. "Ruff, ruff, ruff!"

The driver stops and comes down to pet her. "Well, aren't you a beauty. Come here girl."

She snarls her teeth. "Grrrrrrr."

"Easy girl. I'm not going to hurt you."

Mindy growls louder, "GRRRRRR!" A few laborers surround Mindy, but she grits her teeth to keep them at bay. A crowd of onlookers now curiously observes.

"Maybe it's a stray dog. We should call animal control," one bystander suggests.

"She's probably been abused and feels frightened," another viewer guesses.

"Hey, look over there." A girl from the crowd points to a black and white cat boxing with a construction worker. Screams from the bulldozer operator continue as Frankie takes swipes at him. Other laborers approach upon hearing the commotion but back off not wanting to engage with the angry animals.

"Look what I found!" A young boy runs over to the crowd coddling Shelly in his hands.

His mother scolds him. "That is a baby sea turtle. You are not allowed to disturb them."

"But I think it is lost. It was wandering around in circles," the boy protests.

"Are there more?"

"I don't see anymore, but there are lots of cracked shells," he explains.

"Wait a minute," someone from the crowd speaks up. "It is against the law to build where sea turtles are nesting. This construction crew shouldn't even be here."

"That's right," another voice bellows, waving a newspaper. "There was an article in today's newspaper about this."

The crowd converges like a swarm of bees buzzing toward the construction site. Shouts erupt simultaneously.

"You can't build here."

"This is illegal!"

"You are destroying animal's homes!"

"Get out!"

The dump truck driver recedes as the crowd approaches. He looks for a way out. To his right a wheelbarrow obstructs his path. To the left, an angry man waves his wooden cane with lethal strokes. Directly behind him, the outhouse offers his only refuge. He quickly pivots and fumbles for the handle. The door flings open sending him headfirst into the port-a-potty. Stumbling, he rushes to slam the door shut and flips the latch to occupied. Deep breaths are the only solution to calm the pounding of his heart. Relief is only short-lived. *Bang, bang, bang.* Dizziness overtakes him as the outhouse rocks and rolls mimicking the tumbling waves of the adjacent shoreline.

"You can't hide!"

"Come out you coward!"

An abrupt push sends a week's worth of waste erupting on his shirt and trousers. Sulfur stench permeates his nostrils. Instinctively he covers his nose throwing him off balance. He grips the side of the plastic box, bracing himself for a fall. The outhouse stops short of tipping and flops back into an upright position. An eerie silence fills the air.

Outside, a news van pulls up among the commotion. A reporter weaves her way through the stream of angry citizens. She approaches the portable bathroom and knocks on the door. No response.

She questions him, "Excuse me sir, I'm a reporter with Channel 4 News. Can I speak to you for a moment?" Silence.

"I have a few questions. I'd like to hear your side of the story." Still no response.

Frustrated with the lack of acknowledgment, the mob starts shaking the port-a-potty again. The door bursts open.

"Okay, okay." The foreman steps out with his hands up in the air. He approaches the reporter with slow, exaggerated steps.

"Are you Mr. Weeble? The general construction manager?"

He pauses before nodding his head.

"What are you building here?" The reporter shoves a microphone in his face as the cameraman zooms in on him.

"Uh, it's a luxury accommodation building," he stumbles.

"Is it true you are building a high-rise hotel?" the reporter questions.

"Well yes, there is quite a demand for vacation property along the ocean."

"Do you know that this is a nesting ground for sea turtles?"

The foreman does not answer.

The reporter probes, "The Stillwater Herald reported today that a construction company continues to build even after they discovered the turtle habitat." She pushes the microphone in front of him. Mr. Weeble says nothing.

The young boy approaches the reporter with Shelly. She turns, directing her attention to the blond-haired boy. "Ronald is a young boy who recently found this stranded hatchling. Sea turtles need the light of the moon to guide their way to the ocean," the reporter addresses the camera holding up Shelly.

"But all too often they become disoriented from extraneous lights, such as the ones from this construction site, which has been unlawfully building a high-end hotel. The state has enacted laws to prevent this from happening and encroaching on their natural habitat. What do you have to say for yourself?" She rotates back to Mr. Weeble.

"Uh...umm...well there weren't any turtles here when we started."

"So, you admit that once you discovered the turtles you continued with the project?"

The foreman shoves his hands in his vest and presses his lips together. He glances down and stirs up the sand below by kicking it with the tip of his leather boot. From the corner of his eyes, red lights flash. His shoulders stiffen as the screeching rubber shrieks across the pavement.

The white sedan door slams. A uniformed police officer approaches the crowd. The cluster parts open creating a path for the man. The camera operator quickly shifts focus to the new presence.

"What's going on here?" the pudgy, elder officer asks.

"They are building on the beach where sea turtles are nesting!" someone from the crowd shouts.

"Can I see a copy of your plans?"

"Plans?" His eyes widen.

"Yes, your blueprints. Every building must have proper set back from the ocean."

"Our plans were approved." He lifts up his chest.

"I'd like to see a copy of them."

"City Hall has a copy."

"If you prefer, we can escort you to a lovely room at City Hall."

Mr. Weeble narrows his eyes and grunts. He pivots in slow motion and shuffles his feet, taking his time to stroll to a portable office.

A few minutes later, he returns with a bunch of torn pieces of blue paper. He dumps the pile in the policeman's hands.

"What's this?"

"Our plans. Don't know what happened. I think someone broke into the construction site. When I arrived, they were shredded into pieces."

Frankie and Jagger, now part of the crowd of onlookers, glance at each other and cover their mouths to keep from laughing. They secretly give each other a high five.

The officer pieces the fragments back together. He looks at the piecemealed plan and glances at the site back and forth several times. He takes a step and places the other foot in front touching the heel of the opposite toe. Heel to toe, heel to toe, he makes a rectangle and returns to the starting point.

"These plans don't match what you are building. It's obvious you are encroaching on the natural habitat and are causing harm to the coastal environment."

The policeman approaches Mr. Weeble and places handcuffs around his wrists. "You have the right to remain silent. Anything you say can and will be held against you. If you cannot afford a lawyer one will be appointed to you."

"This isn't fair! The turtles weren't here when we began. Someone must have put them here. We are being framed!" Mr. Weeble squirms and jerks his arms pinching his wrists against the metal cuffs. "Ouch!"

The officer grabs his arm and leads him back through the crowd.

"I am going to sue you for defamation! You have ruined my reputation!" he hollers over his shoulder looking for the television camera.

The camera pans to the journalist. "As you can see the general manager is being taken into custody. I am sure we will be hearing more about this is in the coming days. In the meantime, this construction site will be shut down and a full investigation will take place. We will keep you abreast of details as they come in. For Channel 4 News, this is Amy Manchester."

The crowd erupts in cheers.

"Let's get this little turtle back to the ocean where it belongs," the reporter announces.

The group, which now includes Mindy, Frankie, and Jagger, follows her down to the shoreline. Amy gently places Shelly into the lapping waters. Shelly pauses looking for her friends.

Mindy, Frankie, and Jagger give her an encouraging nod. She flaps a few steps toward the waves and glances back again.

"It's okay Shelly. You are safe now. Go catch up with your family," Frankie reassures.

Mindy and Jagger wave goodbye. She takes a breath and disappears under the incoming tide. She emerges one last time, giving a wink to her friends and dives down letting the current carry her out to her family.

"The Eco Avengers just lost a member." A tear slips down Frankie's face.

"She will always be a part of the Eco Avengers," Mindy reminds. "She will go on to spread the word and help other sea animals."

They stare in silence, taking in the last moments before the outgoing waves disperse into the smooth surface becoming one. The crowd slowly dissolves. A few onlookers place "do not disturb" signs that warn of the sea turtle's nesting grounds.

They glance at each other and nod. Feeling confident their work is done, the trio ventures back toward the road.

"Can we get some breakfast before heading back?" Frankie whines.

Mindy and Jagger simply roll their eyes. But Mindy is already on it.

"Here you go." She hands both Frankie and Jagger a beef jerky stick. Content, they nibble on the snack and begin their journey back home.

DAWN WYNNE

Dawn Wynne is an award-winning author. She
graduated from UCLA with a degree in theater.
After a stint with acting, she became a teacher
where she transformed stories into plays. Her love
of writing and creating characters inspired her to
start writing children's books.

Dawn lives in California with her husband,
daughter, cats, and wild peacocks.

Visit dawnwynne.com for kids' activities, teaching
guides, and resources.

 125

CPSIA information can be obtained
at www.ICGtesting.com
Printed in the USA
LVHW040345160720
660832LV00018B/1314

9 780991 614431